Amy Sparkes is donating 5% of her royalties to Ickle Pickles
(registered charity number 1129763).
Ickle Pickles provides specialist equipment to help
save babies' lives in neonatal units.
To find out more visit: www.icklepickles.org

For Minoti and Ayda –
my inspiration, love and support
– P.C.

For Alex and Elliot – A.S.

First published in 2016
by Scholastic Children's Books, Euston House,
24 Eversholt Street, London NW1 1DB
a division of Scholastic Ltd
www.scholastic.co.uk
London ~ New York ~ Toronto ~ Sydney
Auckland ~ Mexico City ~ New Delhi ~ Hong Kong

Written by Amy Sparkes

Robo-Snot

Illustrated by
Paul Cherrill

SCHOLASTIC

Little Robot had an itch –
His nose began to fizz and twitch,
And as he wondered what to do...

...There came a **very loud**...

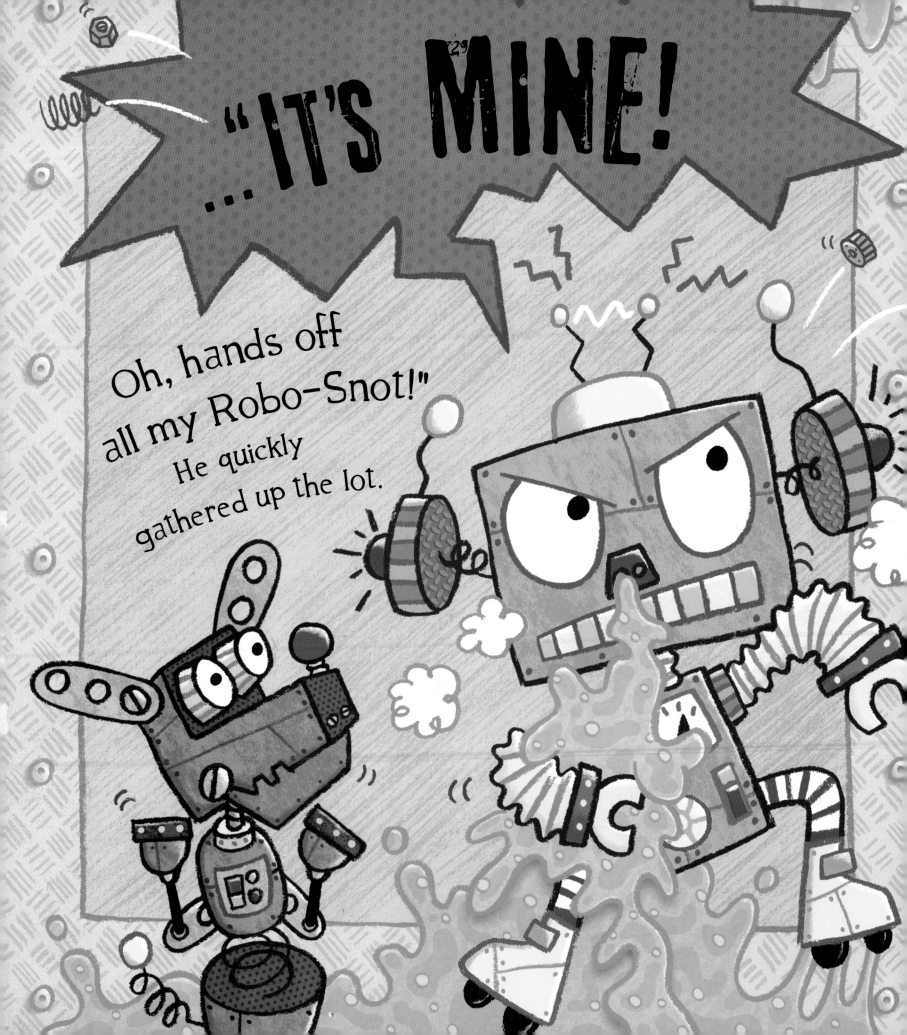

He made the **headlines**,

ROBO NEWS
WHAT A LOT OF SNOT!

starred on screen,

Little Robot
in
ROBO-SNOT
The Movie

SHOWING EVERYWHERE

Royal Decree

Performed before the Robot Queen.

...And soon the **crowd** were sneezing too!

"Ooh!" they cried. "Look what **we've** got! No longer do we need **your** snot!"

All alone, without a friend,
His Robo-fame was at an end.
If things weren't bad enough,
just then...

Oh, what a lot of snotty **MUCK!**"

He squidged and squelched, but rotten luck,

for he was ...well and truly stuck!

Then night rolled in with chilly air,
And scary shapes were everywhere!
Still stuck in all the gloopy goo,
What **could** poor Little Robot do?

"It's scary
in the **dark!**"

he wailed.
He tried to move —
again he failed!

Then two big shadows
loomed nearby.
Which made poor Little Robot cry.
One shadow said,

"Oh, panic not..."

His **robot family** had appeared –
"Oh, **thank you!**"
Little Robot cheered.

His sister said, "Take one of **these**,
To **catch** the snot-slime when you sneeze.
Then use it for some **turbo blows**
To clear the snot out from your nose."

Little Robot said, "I'm sure
No robot has seen this before.
You use it when you go ATISHOO...
I know what! It's called...

...a tissue!"

He grabbed the others by the hand
And said, "I have another plan!"

"We'll all be
For cleaning up